# Words to Know Before You Read

build
clouds
dreary
exclaimed
gracefully
noticed
puddles
shadow
weaving
window

www.rourkeeducationalmedia.com

Edited by Precious McKenzie
Illustrated by Helen Poole
Art Direction and Page Layout by Renee Brady

**Library of Congress PCN Data**

Itsy Bitsy Spider / Colleen Hord
ISBN 978-1-61810-177-8 (hard cover) (alk. paper)
ISBN 978-1-61810-310-9 (soft cover)
Library of Congress Control Number:  2012936777

Rourke Educational Media
Printed in the United States of America,
North Mankato, Minnesota

rourkeeducationalmedia.com

customerservice@rourkeeducationalmedia.com • PO Box 643328  Vero Beach, Florida 32964

# Itsy Bitsy Spider

By Colleen Hord

Illustrated by Helen Poole

Sierra stared out the window as the rain beat against the windowpane. It was a dreary day.

Sierra wanted to play outside, but not in the rain. She liked playing outside when it was sunny.

Shadow tag was one of Sierra's favorite games. She also liked pretending that her shadow was a friend who copied everything she did.

But Sierra could only play the shadow games when the Sun was brightly shining.

As Sierra looked out the window, she noticed an itsy bitsy spider trying to go up the waterspout.

The rain was pouring down so hard it
kept washing the itsy bitsy spider out.

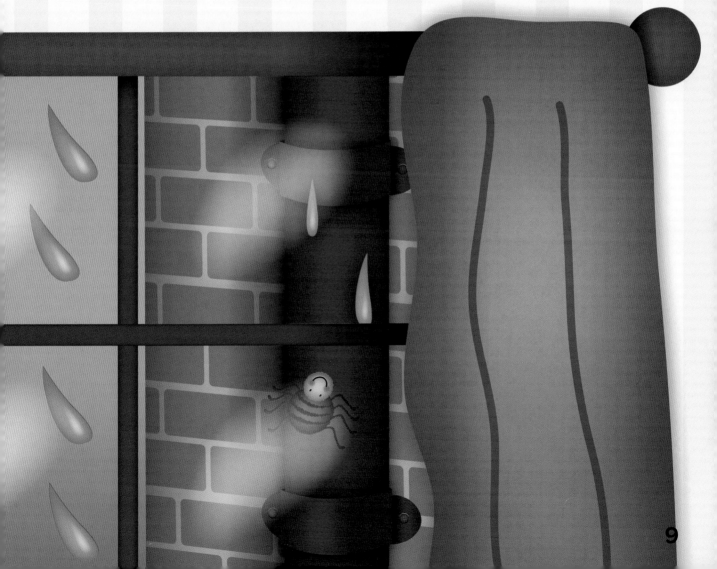

She watched the itsy bitsy spider try over and over again to get to the top of the spout.

No matter how hard the little spider tried, the rain washed the spider out.

"I bet you wish the Sun would come out too," sighed Sierra.

"If the Sun was out, you could see your shadow. You could pretend your shadow was another spider helping you climb to the top."

Sierra watched as the itsy bitsy spider tried one more time to climb up the spout.

Again, the spider
was washed out.

Later that day the rain stopped, the clouds drifted away, and the Sun started to shine.

"I'm going outside to play my shadow games," exclaimed Sierra.

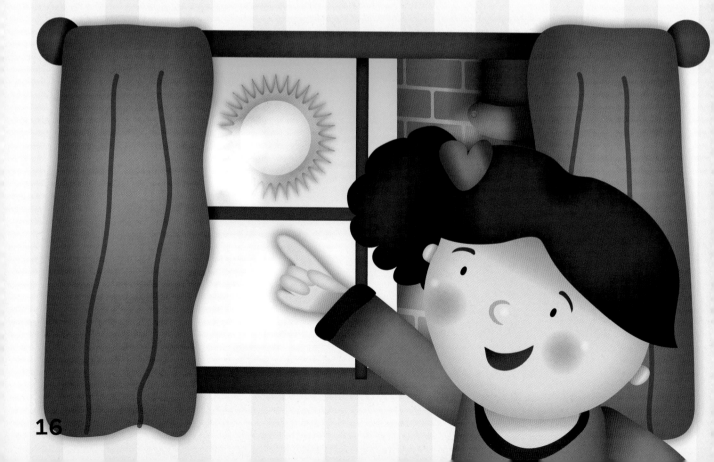

She put on her boots and ran out
the door.

Sierra ran through the puddles. When she splashed, her shadow splashed. When she jumped, her shadow jumped.

Sierra skipped over to the waterspout to check on the spider.

The itsy bitsy spider had finally reached the top of the spout. She was gracefully weaving her web and her shadow was copying everything she did.

"I knew you could do it," Sierra exclaimed. "All you needed was the Sun, and another itsy bitsy spider shadow to help you."

# After Reading Activities

## You and the Story...

What did Sierra like to do on sunny days?
Why couldn't Sierra play her shadow games on a rainy day?
Do you like to play outside in the rain? Explain your answer.
What are some shadow games you could play?

## Words You Know Now...

Take a piece of paper and divide it into three columns. Label the columns: 1 syllable, 2 syllables, 3 syllables.
Write the words below in the correct column.

| | |
|---|---|
| build | noticed |
| clouds | puddles |
| dreary | shadow |
| exclaimed | weaving |
| gracefully | window |

# You Could...Change the Characters in the Story

- Write your own version of Itsy Bitsy Spider using different characters.

- What kind of animal or insect would you use to replace the spider?

- How would the weather influence your characters?

# About the Author

Colleen Hord is an elementary teacher. Her favorite part of her teaching day is Writer's Workshop. She enjoys kayaking, camping, walking on the beach, and reading in her hammock.

**Ask The Author!**
www.rem4students.com

# About the Illustrator

Helen Poole lives in Liverpool, England, with her fiancé. Over the past ten years she has worked as a designer and illustrator on books, toys, and games for many stores and publishers worldwide. Her favorite part of illustrating is character development. She loves creating fun, whimsical worlds with bright, vibrant colors. She gets her inspiration from everyday life and has her sketchbook with her at all times as inspiration often strikes in the unlikeliest of places!